HERBIE'S
BIG
ADVENTURE

JENNIE POH

For Aurelia, Evangeline and baby Theo.
May all your adventures be wild and free.

Published by Curious Fox,
an imprint of Capstone Global Library Limited,
264 Banbury Road, Oxford, OX2 7DY
Registered company number: 6695582

www.curious-fox.com

Printed and bound in China.

HERBIE'S
BIG
ADVENTURE

Herbie was born in the late summer,
just as the first autumn leaves were
beginning to flutter down in the forest.

"MUMMY!" Herbie exclaimed
when he opened his eyes.

"Hello, Herbie," his mother said gently.

Herbie snuggled into her arms.
It felt just right.

Soon Herbie began to play games.

He burrowed in a secret cave...

and *tumbled* in a *tickly* jungle...

and went roly-poly down a steep mountain.

Wheeeee!

Herbie was growing very fast.
Day by day, the little hedgehog
was becoming a big hedgehog.

One day, his mother shared some exciting news.

"Herbie," she said, "you're nearly ready
for your first foraging adventure!"

"Foraging?" Herbie asked.

"To go exploring and find good things to eat," she explained.

Herbie was surprised. "But Mummy, I'm not ready. I'm just a little hedgehog."

"Herbie, you are ready! You can burrow and tumble and sniff! You will go out and explore and come back to me when your adventure is done."

Soon enough, the big day arrived.

"Good luck! Have fun!" his mother called out.

Herbie shivered and took a brave step into the world.

Before he knew it, he was swept up
by a whirling westerly wind.

Whooooooooooooooosh!

Herbie twisted and twirled and landed
in a crisp pile of leaves. CRUNCH!

He quickly began rummaging for things to eat.

"What was I so worried about?"
he wondered. "Foraging is fun!"

Herbie nibbled on an apple core
and felt that everything was just right.

Just as Herbie was about to dig a little deeper,
another swift wind blew into the forest.

Herbie held tightly to a little brown leaf.

The wind carried Herbie and his little brown leaf in a new direction.

Herbie closed his eyes as the air swirled him round and round.

Herbie landed with a POOF.

BRRR! He burrowed upwards and opened his eyes.
Everything twinkled and glistened.

Herbie was chilly and damp. He looked at
the little leaf that had carried him so far.
An idea began to form.

TADA! Herbie's little leaf became a hat!

Herbie climbed his way to the very top
of the world. He was getting sleepy
and wanted to snuggle down for a nap,
but where?

He tried nestling with
a prickly relative...

and squeezing into the
pocket of a troll...

and burrowing under
an owl's wing.

But as hard as he tried, Herbie couldn't find anywhere
to sleep that was as cosy as his mother's arms.

Then Herbie saw a mysterious shape.
As he crept closer and closer,
the shape got bigger and bigger,
until Herbie found himself standing
in the shadow of a great mother
snow bear!

"I am Herbie," the hedgehog said bravely.
"I have been foraging all day, and now I am
looking for a place to rest. I am cold and sleepy."

A small breeze blew, and Herbie saw
the great bear nod and open her arms.
Herbie scurried into them.

The kind snow bear held
the little hedgehog warmly.
It felt just right, and Herbie fell asleep.

Herbie slept soundly all night. In the morning, he felt better.

"Thank you, snow bear!" Herbie said and tumbled out of her arms. At that moment, an enormous easterly wind whistled all around him.

Whoooooooooooooooosh!

The wind blew him all the way back home.

"I just knew you would be home today, Herbie," his mother said.

"You were right, Mummy!" said Herbie.
"I was ready for a big adventure!
But now, being home with you feels
just right."

The End